THIS WALKER BOOK BELONGS TO:

~~Lynette~~ ~~and~~

~~Kirstie~~

~~Chambers.~~

Lee-Anne + Sara

Cook.

3. Fitzjohn Close

Malton.

For Willow, Robin,
Nimrod and Moss
W.M.

For Liam and Simone
B.F.

First published 1986 by
Walker Books Ltd
87 Vauxhall Walk
London SE11 5HJ

Text © 1986 William Mayne
Illustrations © 1986 Barbara Firth

This edition published 1990

Printed in Italy by Graphicom srl

British Library Cataloguing in Publication Data
Mayne, William
Barnabas walks.
I. Title   II. Firth, Barbara
428.6   PE1119
ISBN 0-7445-1352-9

Barnabas walks

Written by

William Mayne

Illustrated by

Barbara Firth

WALKER BOOKS

LONDON

Barnabas walks when all the scholars have left the schoolroom and gone hip-hooraying home.

When the blackboard chalk-dust floats in the setting sun and the desks are still; when the ink is silent and the clock asleep; then Barnabas comes out of his house on a shelf.

Scholars call it a hutch, but to Barnabas it is a house, with a front door, a dining room with hay, a bedroom with straw.

Barnabas opens the front door.

Not every guinea-pig can open his front door. But not every guinea-pig is learning to read.

The scholars can do it, thinks Barnabas. And they are not here all day or every day. They never come on church bell day or football day outside.

Perhaps they come in holiday time when I'm not here, all except Willow and Robin.

Barnabas spends holidays next door at Willow's house. Willow and Robin are sisters that look after him in holiday time.

Nimrod from across the square comes to see him there, without Moss, his dog.

Tonight Barnabas opens his front door.

No one knows he can do it. He does. It creaks, ghostly, ghostly, in the quiet schoolroom.

Barnabas comes out. He goes to look for his reading book. He climbs down from the shelf to the back of a chair.

He climbs to a desk top. Hello, he says to inkwell, and wishes. The ink looks black.

He climbs to the seat of a chair and down a box to the floor. He goes to the middle of the room.

A hungry scholar has left a crumb, a chip, a pea as big as a marble that bounced away from dinner.

Barnabas eats them all carefully. He does not want chewing gum again. It lasted a whole week once, then Willow and Nimrod had to trim his fur with school scissors. He liked being picked up and stroked and rubbing noses, but not the snip scissors.

He finds his book in
a corner no one tidies.

The first page is A,
the next page is B,
after that is C.

Barnabas has looked at the
end to see what happens.

Z happens. He does not know how
they can be so clever. Now he will read the
middle.

He is so busy he does not hear the
schoolroom door open.

He does not hear two scholars come in
for something.

He does not hear them go out with the
thing they wanted.

Barnabas reads all the way to E. He is then hungry.

He walks across the floor. He finds a crisp. He is still hungry. What is one crisp among so many teeth?

He goes home. Up the box, on the seat of the chair, on the desk, on the back of the chair.

Careful about this part, thinks Barnabas, getting up from the floor and starting again.

Lucky not to break a whisker, he thinks, going up the second time.

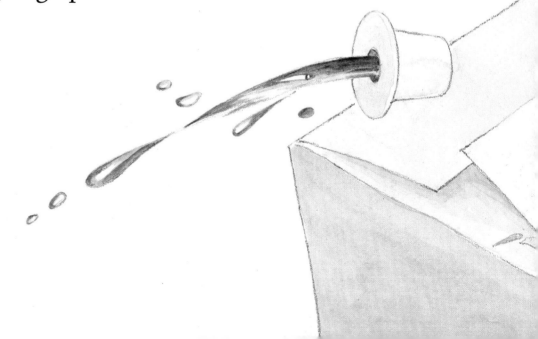

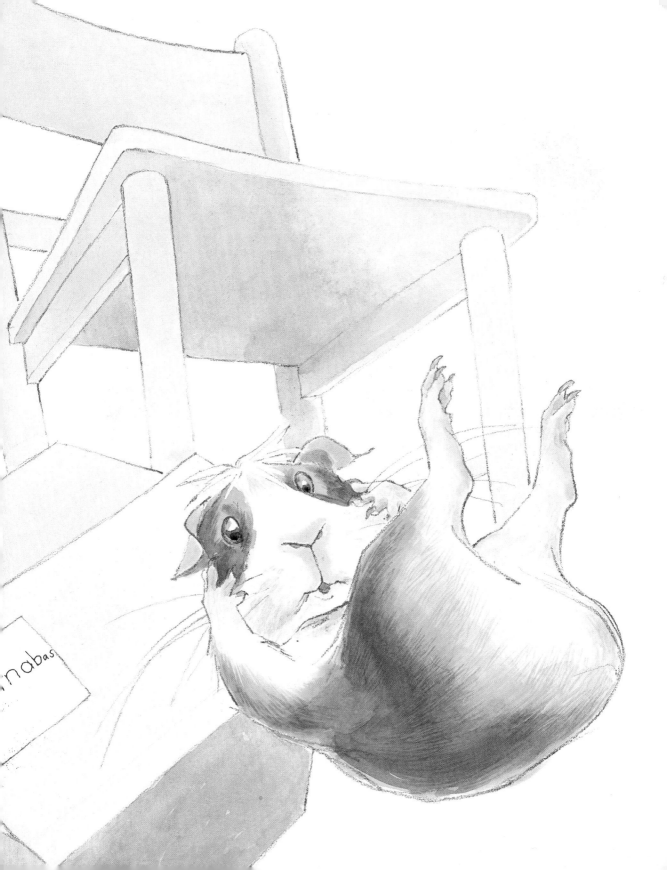

On the shelf again he opens his front door.

He tries to open his front door.

He is where it should be.

How hard it is to do, and all that good food inside.

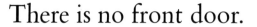

There is no front door.

There is no house. It has gone.

While he read to E scholars came and took his house.

They thought it was a hutch. They thought he was in it. They were being kind because it is holiday now.

But Barnabas was reading D and E, an exciting bit.

Perhaps it was too exciting. I should go
back and read C again, he thinks. Last time
I read it my house was here when I got back.

He looks round the shelf first. No house
is there at all. He sits down where his bed
should be.

No straw. Only the bare, cold, shelf.

In the dining room no hay, no dish of food.

He climbs down, down, down, to the floor.

He finds a stick of straw. He finds a wisp
of hay. One is in the middle of the room,
one is near the door.

He finds a leaf he knows. He was saving
it for supper. It is just outside the
schoolroom door. He tidies it up.

He finds another straw. He knows it. A
guinea-pig knows his own bed.

Now he is in the school yard. No scholars play here tonight.

There is some friendly hay. He sits on it and eats it.

Something comes on to the yard wall and sees him. It licks its lips and stands there very still. A tail switches from side to side. Two eyes watch.

Barnabas does not like the twitching and the watching. He finds a trail of oats and seeds and follows that.

The thing on the wall crouches. It is a
hunting, hungry cat from a ratty farmyard.

Barnabas eats one oat. The cat thinks of
eating Barnabas.

The cat thinks it had better get on with
it, because there are noises nearby.

Willow in the garden shed at home finds
Barnabas is not in bed. Oh, oh.

Robin at the landing window sees him in
the school yard. Oh, oh, oh.

Nimrod, the other side of the road, lets
Moss his dog go for a walk. She has been in
all day, curled up with her puppies. She needs
a run, and her supper.

Robin falls downstairs. Willow trips over her.

The cat is at the edge of the wall.

Now I shall never know what happens between E and Z, thinks Barnabas. I shall only know what happens ever after Z.

The cat is in the air, eyes cruel.

Moss comes into the school yard.

I think HELP comes after E, says Barnabas. He says it once or twice.

He goes on eating. A well-brought-up guinea-pig goes on eating.

Moss runs at the cat. The cat goes away fast, as if it just learned flying.

Dear me, says Moss, and licks Barnabas and picks him up.

HELP says Barnabas again. If it's not one thing it's another. Moss's lick is very sticky.

Supper time, says Moss. She takes him home, and puts him among the puppies, who are all his size and shape and colour.

They are A, B, C, D, and me is E, thinks Barnabas.

Willow and Robin run in and find him.

They all squeak the same, says Nimrod, and gives him back. YELP say puppies, HELP says Barnabas.

He goes back to his house. Willow and Robin dry him dry of lick while he eats a splendid carrot.

Next term, says Barnabas, all the way from E to Z. And perhaps one day the numbers too. But I'm glad Moss can't count.

MORE WALKER PAPERBACKS

THE PRE-SCHOOL YEARS

John Satchwell
& Katy Sleight
Monster Maths
ODD ONE OUT   BIG AND LITTLE
COUNTING   SHAPES   ADD ONE   SORTING
WHAT TIME IS IT?   TAKE AWAY ONE

FOR THE VERY YOUNG

John Burningham
Concept books
COLOURS   ALPHABET
OPPOSITES   NUMBERS

Byron Barton
TRAINS   TRUCKS   BOATS   AEROPLANES

PICTURE BOOKS
For All Ages

Colin McNaughton
THERE'S AN AWFUL LOT OF WEIRDOS IN
OUR NEIGHBOURHOOD
SANTA CLAUS IS SUPERMAN

Russell Hoban
& Colin McNaughton
The Hungry Three
THEY CAME FROM AARGH!
THE GREAT FRUIT GUM ROBBERY

Jill Murphy
FIVE MINUTES' PEACE
ALL IN ONE PIECE

Bob Graham
THE RED WOOLLEN BLANKET
HAS ANYONE HERE SEEN WILLIAM?

Philippa Pearce
& John Lawrence
EMILY'S OWN ELEPHANT

David Lloyd
& Charlotte Voake
THE RIDICULOUS STORY OF
GAMMER GURTON'S NEEDLE

Nicola Bayley
Copycats
SPIDER CAT   PARROT CAT   CRAB CAT
POLAR BEAR CAT   ELEPHANT CAT

Peter Dallas-Smith
& Peter Cross
TROUBLE FOR TRUMPETS

Philippe Dupasquier
THE GREAT ESCAPE

Sally Scott
THE THREE WONDERFUL BEGGARS

Bamber Gascoigne
& Joseph Wright
AMAZING FACTS BOOKS 1 & 2

Martin Handford
WHERE'S WALLY?
WHERE'S WALLY NOW?